THE AUGURY:

The Augury of Destiny

J.C. TAYLOR

JEFFREY C TAYLOR

The Augury of Destiny

Introduction to Drabbles

Introduction to Drabbles

A drabble consists of one hundred words, no more and no less. It can be a complete story, an excerpt or a chapter. A drabble is a lot harder to write as it teaches the ability to be concise. Something most writers avoid! Word counts are king in the world of the author. Admittedly, it still has to be good padding but padding it is nonetheless.

The following is a story that has simply grown, organically, over the past three years since just before lockdown began. It is what I would call a "Flash Novel". In that it's designed to be read when you have just a minute or two between rushing somewhere.

There have been hiccups. I didn't write for almost a year as I found it difficult to do so. Even to the point that the website owner got in contact with me to make sure that I was OK (Still alive and not dead from COVID-19) That was a difficult and scary year as we all watched the death-toll rise, walked eerily silent streets and peered through windows. Suspicious of every person who came to the front door.

Not fun.

Eventually my muse returned and I completed the story. Although the ending needs a bit of work I must admit. It's a bit abrupt. But, so was Dune and apparently that's a classic. So here's hoping that you, the reader, enjoys the ride.

Jeff

2022

Magic

"Magic I hear you say? You do understand what it is don't you?"

The boy shook his head.

"Hmm... Magic is how the Universe works. It is, at its simplest, the manipulation of reality." The old man stood. "One moment there is no staff in my hand... the next?" The air pinched together, leaving behind a tall staff of white ash. "There is a staff. But you must already know some of this, even if you do not have the words to explain it. Otherwise you would not be before me. Your father sent you to me did he not?"

A Simple Wooden Toy

The boy sat before the old man, and presented him with a simple wooden toy. A dog. The old man took it, and peered closely at it.

"You took this?"

The boy shook his head. "Made it."

"Hmm..." Rumbled the old man. "There is a price that must be paid when using magic. Especially powerful creation magics. How long did you sleep?"

"Two days." The boy replied.

"I must admit to being impressed boy. Making something, even this small, would knock me out for the best part of a week. You do need training. You'll stay here with me now."

The Neutron Oracle

"It's been a while since I've had an apprentice boy. I'm not getting any younger, but even I need some guidance." The boy looked quizzically at him. "We need to go on a short journey, and consult the Oracle."

"Oracle?"

"The Neutron Oracle. It's two days journey into the mountains. I'd prefer to stay down here on the coast, but I think we need to go. The mountain air is not good on these old bones of mine, but it's far better on my lungs."

"I don't have any travel clothes."

"Then let's go shopping boy, and spend some money."

Shopping at The Travellers Store

"Ah, master Tellerick. What can we do for you today?"

"I need a new set of camping gear for this one. Boots, mat, tent..."

"Clothes..." Whispered the boy.

"Oh, and clothes. And a waterproof cape."

"Going on a long trip master Tellerick?" Asked the shop owner as he busied himself with gathering what was immediately to hand.

"Off to see the Oracle on the slopes of Milloran mountain. We'll be gone for some time."

"Oh? Will anyone be taking on your duties while you are away?"

"Master Omui will be in attendance. If you need anything please talk to him."

Travelling Is Uncomfortable

The boy stood outside the shop as a newly minted traveller beneath a, shin length, waxed cape. Behind him, his backpack gave him the appearance of a hunchback, while the hood flopped down over his face so he could only see the floor from its dark recess.

"It's heavy" He grumbled.

The mage stood next to him. "It will get heavier boy. But also lighter. Travelling is never a comfortable business."

"Isn't there a train?"

"Not into the mountains boy! Good grief, it's dangerous up there! There is one to the foothills though, you will be glad to know of."

A Guard... A Guide...

There was a hint of rain in the air as the two walked further into town.

"Where are we going now?" Asked the boy, as the hustle and bustle increased around them.

"First, to a tavern."

"You want to drink?"

"A swift pint won't go amiss, I will admit. But we have another purpose."

The boy looked up at the mage quizzically. "We do?"

"Aye boy. We need a guide, and a guard. We will do well if we get both in one."

"But I thought..."

"I told you boy. The mountains are a very, very, dangerous place to be."

A Pint Of Gribbley's Please...

The tavern went quiet as master Tellerick strode imperiously in through the door. Followed by a shy boy, who quietly closed the door behind them.

"Get me a pint of Gribbley's boy. I need to talk to the guild rep." He pointed at the thin representative sitting quietly in one corner, holding a book and looking mildly bored.

The boy approached the bar, and clambered up a stool after propping his backpack against it. He pulled his hood back. "Master Tellerick would like a pint of Gribbley's please."

The barkeep looked at him. "I heard." He started pulling the pint.

Payment In Full...

The adventurer's guild rep looked up at Tellerick over the top of his half-moon glasses. "And what can I do for you today master Tellerick?"

"I need a guard to travel to see the Oracle." The rep sighed heavily. "Guild payment in full, up front."

"What?"

"Guild policy changed last week from payment-on-delivery." Tellerick sighed, and reached for his money pouch.

"How much?"

"The only guild member available at the moment is Madam Whitesnow. She's by the big fireplace. She's a gold a day." Tellerick glowered at him.

"Is she good?"

"Yes sir. Of course she is."

Prices These Days

Tellerick grudgingly paid the rep for two weeks, and signed the hiring document that also required additional payment should it take longer than usual. Then there was travel insurance on top of that, even though the rep thought whoever might attack would regret it.

His copy of the documents in hand, he walked over to the boy who was waiting patiently by a table.

Tellerick sat, and took a heavy swig of his ale. "This is proving to be an expensive trip. Prices have gone up so much since I last left the cottage." He lifted his tankard. "Even this!"

The Other Bar

The boy sipped his water, as Tellerick finished his pint. "I really should visit the pub more often."

"Father comes here a lot."

"Oh, does he now? I shan't ask how he can afford it. Come, boy. Let's find our new colleague. The rep said she was by the big fireplace." The boy looked around. "It's round the back boy. Come on!" Tellerick picked up his bag, as the boy hastily drank the rest of his water.

The tables and chairs, in the other bar, were much, bigger than where they had been sitting. And for very good reason too.

Sometimes You Get What You Pay For

Tellerick suddenly understood why his new hire was just so expensive as they turned the corner to see the fireplace.

A high backed chair had been turned towards the fire, and a pair of huge, black and white, hind paws were dominating the footrest. A gallon tankard sat on the table next to the chair. And the tip of a striped tail twitched idly from the side.

"Madam Whitesnow?"

"Who's askin'?" Growled the ten foot warrior tigress.

Tellerick presented his papers, and watched as they disappeared into the giant paws. She delicately read through. "You paid travel insurance as well?"

Introductions

Kralla Whitesnow stood up, and handed back the mage's papers.

"Nice to meet you Master Tellerick." She smiled, showing her enormous canines, and raised a paw-hand to shake. Tellerick was suddenly reminded what it was like to be a child in a grown-ups world as his hand was engulfed in a claw laden paw.

"And who might you be kitling?" She knelt down on, one knee, to look at the boy; although it didn't make her seem any less intimidating.

"My name is William."

"Hello. I'm Kralla Whitesnow. Are you coming with us then?"

"Yes Ma'am. I am."

Open Ended Contract?

Kralla sat back down after pulling across two, human sized, chairs. "Your contract isn't open ended master Tellerick." She said, before sipping from her beer.

"You are... A little expensive."

"That's the guild. Don't worry about any extended durations. Shit happens, and I'm a professional. As long as the basics are sorted, that's the important thing. Anything above what you've paid already is at my discretion, not the guild's."

Tellerick relaxed. "That is good to know madame."

"Please!" She smiled. "You have to call me Kralla. I prefer to be on first-name terms. I'm not a fan of titles.

Rumours Of Trouble In The Mountains

"So master Tellerick. Your papers are signed, sealed and in order. Where are we going, and when?" Kralla daintily slurped at her beer.

"Tomorrow morning. We're going to the oracle in the mountain."

Kralla frowned. "You do know that there's been reports of undead up there recently? I read in the guild newsletter about an attack on a village in the foothills." Tellerick sighed, and nodded heavily.

"Yes. I saw that this morning when we came into town. However, the oracle is well protected where it is. We are going straight there and back. So it should be quick'n easy."

Additional Services

The morning was cool and fresh as Master Tellerick, and William, entered the courtyard after a travellers breakfast. Kralla was growling at a pack rat over prices.

"Good morning mistress Whitesnow."

"Ah, Master Tellerick. I'm just negotiating some additional help. This is Skaran." The rat nodded at them politely. "He will be joining us with some extra supplies"

"Extra?"

"All part of my Services Master Tellerick. There will also be an old friend of mine joining us along the way. A Paladin."

"Really..? I..."

"I'm sorry Master Tellerick, but the undead really give me the heeby jeebies." She shivered violently.

On the road

Kralla and Master Tellerick strode next to each other on the road to Tallra's Pike. Tellerick kept glancing up at the tigress, an expression of vague amusement on his face.

"Is there something wrong Master Tellerick? Is there something on my face?"

"No. I'm sorry Kralla. It's not often I travel, let alone with a tigress wearing a hat."

She adjusted the huge, floppy, summer hat a little. "It keeps the sun off. White fur means sunburn, as much as no fur."

Tellerick smiled. "Fair point. About our new colleague...."

"Ah," She nodded. "Yes. Tamryn is an old, old friend."

On The Road #2

"Is he..?"

"Yes, Master Tellerick. He's a honey badger to be clear. I'm surprised at you Tellerick. I never pegged you as discriminatory. The sundering of species wasn't our fault you know."

"I know. Please accept my apologies. I am a grumpy old man."

Kralla playfully punched him in the arm. "Apology accepted. Best keep the grump to yourself old man. Don't go teaching the boy bad habits."

"I trust that you will put me straight if I do that Kralla. I'll need you to take care of the boy if anything happens as well... Return him to his father..."

Dribbling Noses

"I'm not going!" Sniffed Tamryn, before blowing his nose. "I've got a cold."

"But..? We need you!" Implored Kralla. "You're the best! As far as I know, those mountains are crawling with undead." She shivered violently. "You know they creep me out!"

"Kralla, you're a big lass. You should get a grip." Tamryn sipped his hot toddy.

"But... but..."

"Take the boy if you must. I'm getting too old for this crap anyway. Why do you think I live here at the monastery? Practice? No. It's nice, quiet and above all, hallowed ground. Not a skeleton, or zombie in sight!"

A Sniffling Introduction

"Barnabas! Get your mangy tail in here! And where's my top up!" Shouted Tamryn, before collapsing in a fit of coughing and finally blowing his nose as noisily as possible.

A young fox walked in brandishing a steaming, and very alcoholic smelling bowl. "Your refill master Tamryn..." Barnabas stopped at the towering site of Kralla. "Er..."

"Stop goggling boy!" Tamryn slurped at his fresh drink, before draping a towel over his head. "Kralla, this here is Barnabas. Barnabas, this is Kralla, you're going with her into the mountains for a bit."

Barnabas' mouth dropped open. "But master! I'm not allowed!"

Time To Get Your Feet Wet...

Tamryn pulled the towel from his head. "Boy, you need to be out in the field at some point. I can't think of anyone better than Kralla here to be out there with you."

"But Master! The church..."

"Pah! Most of those old fogies haven't been out of the monastary in fifty years! Let alone go down to the village once in a while, or go out preaching. You're young, you've had training. Now it's time to get your feet wet."

"But master, there are rumours of..."

"Poppycock and balderdash boy! If there's undead in those mountains, I'll eat my..."

Leaving home

Barnabas looked uncomfortable as he hefted his heavy backpack onto his shoulders.

"I don't like this master..."

"Oh stop whining boy!" Said Tamryn, before messily blowing his nose again. "You'll be fine! Kralla here is more than capable, and so is master Tellerick. You're just going for spiritual support. Nothing more."

"If you say so master."

"Now; you've refilled your flask with holy water?"

"Yes master."

"And symbols?"

"I've got a big one, a bag of small ones and my book, master."

"Good. Now put this in your bag as well." He handed Barnabas a small bone wrapped in feathers.

A Summer Night's Chat.

Kralla poked at the fire with a stick. Embers floated up in the convection currents, dancing with the fireflies that winked in and out of existence in the warm summer night. "So when are you going to start teaching young William, Master Tellerick?"

"I am. Well, patience at the moment."

"All you've done is teach him some basic travelling skills. That's not magic."

"No. They are life lessons that he's going to need."

"If he has the power you say he has, he's going to need some way to defend himself. Don't you think?"

"Well... You do have a point."

Morning Light

The morning dew clung to the grass, glistening in the early morning sun. Kralla was busy re-lighting the fire with the wood gathered by Skaran. Soon the smells of a hearty breakfast filled the air.

Tellerick beckoned to William who'd just finished packing his backpack.

"What do you know of the elements boy?"

"Fire, water, air and earth?"

"Your father teach you that?" Said Tellerick, resisting the urge to hold his head in his hands.

"Yes sir."

Tellerick sighed heavily. "Kralla was right. I need to teach you some basics, and sooner rather than later. Right. This is important..."

Bad Brush

As they walked, Tellerick guided his charge in the creation of soap bubbles from nothing. They floated on the breeze, little balls of glistening colour.

Kralla, Skaran and Barnabas trailed behind the pair.

"So... Barnabas... Your, er, tail..."

"It's a skin condition!" He moaned. "Everyone thinks I've got mange!"

Kralla, fiddled with her hat. "Sorry, I had to ask..."

Barnabas sighed. "I wish it was a bushier brush..." He reached into a pocket and brought out a small jar. "I have cream for it! Master Tamryn said it will go away in a few weeks. It's not really my fault."

A Bad Smell...

The smell came first, and tickled evilly at Barnabas's sensitive nose. Acrid and rotting, as Barnabas came to, it also woke Skaran the pack-rat...

"You smell that?" Hissed Skaran. His whiskers, shivering glass in the moonlight. Barnabas took a deeper sniff and his eyes shot wide open. He quickly covered his muzzle with his hands, leaned into the bushes behind him and threw up as quietly as possible. "I'll take that as a yes then." Skaran quickly rose, and trod silently over to Kralla. "Mistress Kralla! Wake! We have company!"

"Eh? What?"

"Company, mistress. Fairly bad company I'd say..."

Way to go...

"Master Tellerick... Awaken! We have..." Skaran crinkled his nose. "Master Tellerick?" Tellerick broke wind as he moaned awake.

"Eh? What is it Skaran?"

"Oh my Goddess Master Tellerick! What have you been eating?" Skaran held his paws tightly over his nose.

Tellerick sniffed. "Whooh! Was that me? Very sorry Skaran. My insides are not used to all that rich campfire food."

The others looked on. "I guess I should sleep down-wind from the rest of you eh?"

"Now I know why there's so much undead in these mountains." Sniggered Kralla.

"Well, that's one way to turn them..." Said Barnabas.

A Battle Starts

Tellerick felt something sharp, and looked down at the rusty sword protruding from his chest. Red velvet blood dripped from its edge onto the floor. His vision darkened, and closed in as he collapsed to the floor.

In the darkness he felt a bony foot push into the small of his back and a tug as the blade was pulled from him.

Around him he heard the dull chink sound of sword on sword. He could still breath, but he had no feeling in the lower part of his body. Consciousness faded away, as he bled out onto the floor.

Engagement in the Forest of Mallarium

The Skeleton warrior slid its rusty sword from Tellerick's back and raised it to strike again as Kralla's roar of fury split the sudden quiet. Her sword slammed down through the undead warrior shattering bone, more like a hammer than a blade, as it went.

Quickly, Skaran grabbed at Tellerick's prone body and heaved him out of the way as more undead entered the, now blazing, firelight.

Behind Kralla, Barnabas grabbed at his bag and yanked at the slipknot holding a pouch to it. Paws shaking, he pulled out a small twist of paper and threw it into the fire...

A Smart Move

Blinding light filled the small glade as Barnabas, on his knees in prayer, shouted out "Unbind!" The remaining skeletons stopped, then collapsed where they stood.

Barnabas rushed to the edge of the firelight, and started throwing up.

Kralla sighed, and knelt next to Tellericks prone body. "Skaran?" The packrat smiled.

"He'll be fine. Clever old bastard. He's been teaching the boy healing magic." He pulled a blanket over William, who was now curled fast asleep next to Tellerick.

"Oh thank the gods!" She turned, and walked over to Barnabas who was wiping his last meal from his muzzle and whiskers.

Queasy Fox

Kralla bent over Barnabas and helped him to his feet. "Are you alright?" Barnabas nodded.

"Yes. Sorry, I'm. Er... They make me feel so sick. I'm really sensitive to bound spirit creatures like those." He gestured at the piles of bones, rusty swords and rotten armour.

"So, wait... Are you telling me that when you get close..."

"Yeah... I start throwing up. It was one of the reasons I was at the monastery."

"One?"

Barnabas sighed heavily, and took a swig at the water bottle Kralla had in her giant paw.

"Yeah... There's another reason..."

"Oh?"

"They like me... Lots!"

That Explains a Lot

"What do you mean? They like you?" Kralla scowled, as realisation dawned.

"Same way you like catnip probably." came the mumbled reply from fox.

"So, wait... You're like... Catnip for the undead!?"

"Yeah. Apparently I, and I'm quoting here... Shine."

Kralla buried her face in her palm. "Why that old bastard!" She growled. "He deliberately... Hang on. If you're undead-nip then why haven't we seen any until now? We're only a day, or so, away from the Oracle. Did Tamryn give you something? Cast a spell on you?"

"Oh, wait! He gave me this before we left. Maybe that's..?"

We Have To Move...

"We can't stay here." Announced Kralla, stepping away from the fox and the fetish he was brandishing.

Skaran looked up from Tellerick and the boy. "We can't move Master Tellerick yet. I can still feel the magic healing him."

"We have to Skaran. We need to keep moving now. Turns out young Barnabas here is a lighthouse for the undead. They stumbled across us this time, but now they'll probably start hunting us..."

"But Kralla!"

"No! We have to move." She gathered up her sleeping roll and tied it to her pack. "We have to move as soon as possible."

Moonlit Travel

The group quickly gathered up the camp. "I'll take Master Tellerick. Barnabas, you take the boy." Kralla slid her paws gently under the sleeping mage, and lifted him easily into the air. Barnabas made a sling from a scarf, and picked up William, using the scarf as a support.

"Skaran, lead the way. You do know the way don't you?" Skaran nodded at Kralla.

"This way..." He turned, and headed deeper into the forest, an animal track at his feet.

The half-moon lit the ground with dappled shade. Silver eyed, they moved as quickly, and as silently, as possible.

A Few Miles

Having put a good few miles between them, and their last campsite, the group stopped to rest for the remainder of the night.

Barnabas put William down onto a sleeping mat, and then pulled a small bottle from his backpack. Quickly he circled the clearing, sprinkling water from the bottle and muttering words of power beneath his breath. Finally he sat down.

"That should keep us from prying eyes until morning." Kralla patted him on the back.

"Good work. For someone who's not been out travelling before, you're doing well."

He looked sorrowfully at Tellerick. "Not well enough I think."

Sweet Tea

Master Tellerick opened his eyes, and immediately grabbed his aching chest. Beneath him, he could feel the hole as new skin touched the sleeping mat below. He took a deep, juddering breath of cold, damp, morning air before pushing himself upright.

"Welcome back to the land of the living Master Tellerick." Skaran proffered a steaming mug of tea. "You were lucky Master William got to you in time."

Tellerick took hold of the tea, and took a sip. Skaran had put too much honey in it, and it tasted... glorious. "How is he?"

Skaran pointed. "Still sleeping."

"And the others?"

Waking from a night of running

A white tiger ear fluttered, as Kralla awoke to a quiet conversation on the chill autumn morning air. The smell of a damp-wood fire permeated the camp as she propped herself up on one arm.

Across from her, the welcome sight of Master Tellerick nursing a tin mug of steaming tea greeted her.

"A good morning Master Tellerick." She growled, pushing back the blanket.

"And to you Mistress Whitesnow..." Tellerick seemed faintly embarrassed. "Thank you for saving my life."

"Thank your student Master Tellerick, not me." She took a mug of tea from Skaran. "We need to talk undead..."

Last Night...

Once Barnabas was awake, and leaving William to sleep, the group sat around the fire to discuss the events of the previous night...

Tellerick started. "We all thought it was a rumour about the undead, but last night made it very clear. There is something dreadfully wrong here."

"Agreed Master Tellerick." Nodded Kralla. "But that was no random encounter last night. That was a patrol."

"Surely not! That would mean..." Exclaimed Barnabas.

Kralla couldn't help herself, and growled menacingly. "There is a controlling force here somewhere."

"We cannot deviate Kralla." Tellerick sipped his tea. "We must get to the Oracle."

Education

Kralla frowned. "Why is it so important to get to the Oracle, other than it may be a place of safety?"

Tellerick stared into his tea. "We need to get William there, and present him. I believe that he is a nexon of power."

"A what now?" Said Kralla.

"A mage of extraordinary ability." Mumbled Skaran. "If William is indeed what you say he is Master Tellerick, then your teachings are more important than ever."

They all looked at the rat somewhat surprised. "What? I may be a humble pack rat, but I am quite capable of reading a book."

The Fetish

"Skaran is right. Fortunately the mage arts are not as attractive, as those of the believers, to the undead." Tellerick looked pointedly at Barnabas.

"That is a little unfair Tellerick." Growled Kralla. "Barnabas wasn't to know, and the rumours of the undead wandering the mountain were just that. Rumours."

"No Kralla. Master Tellerick has a point. I'm a beacon to the undead." He pulled the fetish from a pocket. "Master Tamryn thought ahead though, and gave me this. It's a cloaking fetish. As long as I have this, I will be invisible to the evil lurking here in the mountains."

The Tree Line

The early morning mist clung to the edge of the forest. Hugging bush, and tree. Waiting for the late summer, early autumn sun to burn it away. Far above a thicker cloud-bank grasped the mountain with a firm, and resolute, grip. Defying the sun. Betwixt the two lay the open ground of the scrublands that led into the dead scree of the mountain tall itself.

"I don't like this. This is ambush country." Growled Kralla.

"But you knew it was here, right?" Barnabas almost squeaked, as the group peered, from the tree line.

"Yes. Still don't like it though..."

We All Glow

"It makes no difference to the undead if we move during the light, or the dark. We all glow to them just the same."

Kralla's head snapped round. "What do you mean we all glow to them?" Barnabas flinched, as she growled at him.

"OK. Maybe some more than others, but the living all glow somewhat to them. We can't avoid it."

Kralla's eyes narrowed. "Someone is doing very well right now."

Tellerick laid a hand on her shoulder. "Now Kralla..." Suddenly she snapped back the other way, and snarled menacingly at Tellerick, before grasping her head with a paw.

I Don't Feel So Good...

"I don't feel so good." Kralla shook her head, as her companions scrambled backwards. "Head feels... Foggy." She stumbled forwards.

"Oh shit." Hissed Barnabas. Tellerick was already reaching into his bag, muttering under his breath.

Further along the tree line, a knight stepped out. The slight breeze carried the stench of rot, and rust, as it turned towards the party. It raised an arm, pointing its longsword straight at Barnabas.

The screech cut through the quiet morning; metal claws on a blackboard. Loud, long and blood curdling before ceasing.

All sound stopped. Everything was enveloped in a cloying, thick, silence.

Protection

Tellerick stood, grabbing Barnabas by the scruff of the neck and standing him upright, while throwing a cloud of glittering dust above the group. It descended around them, forming an unnatural, glittering dome of sparkling white.

"Crafty bastards." Tellerick's voice was deafening after the all encompassing silence. "We must've tripped a watch spell. Skaran, grab Kralla and get her in close. I don't know how long this is going to last." He turned to Barnabas. "Protection spell. Now boy! Or we're all going to be joining their ranks."

Barnabas sprang into action, taking a symbol of faith from his bag.

The Dome of Sound

Skaran dropped his pack, and ran to Kralla who'd stumbled away holding her head. Outside the sparkling dome of dust the silence was deafening, making his own thoughts seem like shouting. He grabbed at her from behind as she tumbled into the scrub. "God's damnit Kralla, you're heavy!" Grunting, he dragged her back to the others.

Back inside the dome sound returned, along with some of Kralla's senses. "Let go of me rat." She suddenly snarled. Skaran, tensed and let go as she turned and knelt. "My apologies Skaran, that was uncalled for. I don't know what came over me."

More Join the Fray

Barnabas tried desperately to concentrate, as he spied another six skeletal warriors emerge from the treeline. They gathered next to the knight that had cast the spell of silence, and turned, as one, towards Barnabas. Or at least that was how it felt. The fox shouted the end of the protection spell at the top of his voice, before plunging the iron symbol deep into the ground. The air changed subtly, taking on the oily sheen of a soap bubble around them.

"I don't know how long this is going to keep them out..." He whispered hoarsely to Master Tellerick.

Lighting the Beacon

Tellerick placed a hand on Barnabas's shoulder. "You're not done yet lad. I can't turn the undead. That's your job. But we can give you all the support you need."

"But... The protection? I thought..."

Tellerick laughed out loud as the Knight, and its cohorts, stomped towards them.

"Lad. Take a deep breath. The old badger wouldn't have sent you with us if he didn't think you'd last more than five minutes. But we need to make the most of you." He opened the palm of his hand, and beckoned. "Hand it over now. We need to light a beacon."

And More Came...

Barnabas reached inside his tunic, and pulled out the tiny fetish that Master Tamryn had snuck into his pocket when they left the monastery.

"Are you sure?"

Tellerick nodded, and Barnabas dropped the fetish into his open hand.

"Don't worry. I'll keep it safe. Not to mention... If it was powerful enough to hide you from them, then I've just become completely invisible. And that is a mistake they are too dead to regret." Barnabas nodded.

Behind them Kralla stood, and unsheathed her giant twin swords. "I hope you know what you're doing Master Tellerick. I count another twenty undead."

Breathe Lad...

Rust and rot emerged from the tree line on both sides of Tellerick's party.

The undead, of armies lost to time and myth, dragged themselves out of the sickly earth. Many of the skeletons were partial, some fresher than others. Their water logged skin hanging from their bones, and ancient leather straps barely held their armour to their spindled and cracked bodies.

The Knight that had seen them first, held its chipped sword high and screeched before charging forwards.

"The protection spell can't handle this many!" Cried Barnabas.

"Breathe lad. I'm going to give you a bit of a boost."

Whites of their Eyes

Kralla and Skaran looked nervously at the charging horde of undead skeletons. "Is this a 'White of their eyes' thing Tellerick? Because if it isn't, it was nice knowing you."

"Kralla, now is not the time... Barnabas, when I say, cast a turn undead. I won't lie, this is probably going to hurt. A lot. But me, more than you. Alright?" Barnabas nodded as Tellerick placed both hands on his shoulders. "We need to get as many in close as we can. Kralla, Skaran, you will need to clean up. I'm not going to be able to help you out."

Flashes of Protection

The Knight reached the protection barrier and brought its sword down with the strength only the dead can weald. It flashed brilliant white. Another flash came as an arrow bounced off.

"Shit! They've got an archer with them." Growled Kralla.

"I see it." Skaran pointed. "It's there."

"First on the list for clean up. It'll likely hang back. Keep your eyes on it Skaran."

Behind the pair Barnabas was saying the preamble to his casting, and behind him Tellerick was doing the same.

"I hope this works Skaran."

"Aye Kralla. I hope this works too. I'm too pretty to die."

Divine Light

Like ants attacking an intruder to their nest the undead swarmed over the shield of protection, blocking the sky and plunging them all into deathly darkness.

Gripping the shoulders of Barnabas with all his strength, Master Tellerick uttered the final words of his spell beneath his breath "Power of two"

In front, Barnabas raised his symbol of faith High above and whispered... "Turn"

The symbol blazed with a divine white light. Almost a liquid, it bubbled out; seething, penetrating and expanding. The Dome of Protection shattered into nothingness and rained dust, rust and powdered leather down upon the party beneath.

Pack Rat Ball

Kralla eyed the archer in the distance and grabbed Skaran's backpack, with him still wearing it.

"Grab your tail. Arms in. Legs in." Deflecting another arrow with her buckler, she roared and threw Skaran straight at the skeletal soldier with all her might.

The impact knocked the breath out of Skaran, but it was more than enough to knock the archer onto its back. Frantically, fighting off the skeleton's grabbing claws, Skaran dismembered the bones. Scattering them as he went.

Kralla turned to the remaining soldiers that had hung back. Pulling her twin scimitars from her back she roared again.

The Remains of the Day

Kralla charged at the remaining skeletal warriors. Her twin swords were useless as cutting and slashing weapons in this case, but as crushing bludgeons?

The first skeleton exploded in a mist of chards and broken bones, as she parried the next, and danced into the middle of the group. Swords singing, and Kralla roaring at the top of her voice, she span and dodged. Landing crushing blows, she quickly whittled them down in a breathless tornado of spinning swords and curses.

Panting heavily, as the last one went down, she turned back to her charges and stamped back to them.

Breather

"Are there any more?" Snarled Kralla as she arrived back with the others. Everyone was covered in dust, powdered rust and leather dust.

"Barnabas is making sure now." Replied Skaran, wiping his nose and cleaning his whiskers.

"There's nothing for miles." Said Barnabas, finishing his chant. "Thank goodness. I'm not sure that we can do that again too soon."

"Aye... That was more than a bit rough." Said Skaran.

"Rough? Rough!?" Snapped Kralla. "Where the hell did that number of undead come from? Where did that trip spell come from? We have a very serious decision to make." She growled.

An Answer to a Question

"And what might that be?" Whispered Tellerick. His face grey with dust and weary from channelling so much energy. "Whether we turn around and go back down the mountain?"

"We do have master William to consider." Said Skaran.

"We are here for him Skaran. We're not returning until we have seen the Oracle."

"Need I impress upon you the folly of ignoring what we just encountered Tellerick?" Replied Kralla as she paced the camp.

"I am not ignoring it Kralla." Sighed Tellerick. "But we must carry on..."

"I am contracted to escort you. But I don't have to like it."

From Bad to Worse to...

Tellerick sighed heavily. "I understand that our recent luck has been poor, and we are likely going to push it further than anyone would like to. However, we need to carry on!"

"Your commitment is commendable Master Tellerick, but you know that I have to raise this. It's my job to keep you all safe. That's what you paid me to do, and I will do it." Replied Kralla.

"Bravo!" Came a voice from farther up the mountainside. "Bravo! To you."

They all turned towards the voice. "Can I suggest that things have gone from bad to worse to... Boned?"

The Lord of Misery

A figure stepped out of the mist clinging to the upper part of the mountainside, stubbornly resisting the sun's power.

"Apologies, brave adventurers. I should announce myself." The figure threw its arms wide, revealing bone clawed hands wrapped in parchment skin. "I am the Lord of Misery. His unholiness, Lord Marakel." It screeched before a withered arm swung about to point directly at the group. "And you are not only trespassing, but you have somewhat upset me by destroying my local forces. What the bloody hellfire are you doing on my mountain?!"

"Uh oh." Mumbled Skaran, quickly gathering his things.

The Scent of Power

The figure drifted closer, just above the ground, before stopping in front of the group.

"I also smelt..." Marakel pointed at Barnabas. "You! I can smell your power. It is masked, but I can still..."

"Back away creature." Snarled Kralla.

"Silence!" Screeched Marakel. "You will bow in my presence!" It pointed a bony finger at the ground, pulling the parchment skin into a grimace of a smile.

They all felt the power of Marakels compulsion grip them like a vice. Crushing them to the ground. Kralla grunted, as she resisted.

"I said KNEEL!!"

Kralla dropped to one knee and bowed.

Surprise!

Marakel drifted over to Barnabas. "You... You... Ah..." It reached into Barnabas' clothes and brought the fetish into the light. "Here, yes..." It brought the fetish to its nose and sniffed deeply. Suddenly, eyes ablaze, it drifted back. "I smell Tamryn!"

"Guilty as charged." Came the voice of the old badger from behind them. "It's been too long Marakel! Who's been a naughty lich?"

"You!" Hissed Marakel

"Don't make me, make you, release them. Let them go. They have a different destiny. You and I on the other hand... We need to talk. I need to know why you're here."

Not Now Kitty!

Marakel looked at the group. "It seems, Tamryn, that I have quite a good bargaining chip in play."

Tamryn laughed. "Seriously Marakel?" He turned back to the tree-line. "Lads!?" Through the brush came the monks of the Order of Sadrymar.

Marakel glowered at Tamryn as he turned back to face the Lord of Misery.

"You were always a downer Tamryn. Never any fun at all." He graciously bowed, flinging his arms out wide.

Suddenly, the weight pressing them to ground disappeared and Kralla bunched to pounce.

"Ah! No! Kitty! Maybe we will meet again after my words with Tamryn."

Time To Leave Now

Tellerick placed a firm hand on Kralla's shoulder. "This isn't our fight Kralla. We need to get out of the way. Now!" She snarled at the ancient figure.

"Oh, I'm sure we will meet again oh Queen of Swords." Smirked Marakel. "Maybe next time we can waltz on the battlefield?"

"Stop goading her Marakel." Shouted Tamryn. "You still haven't told me what you're doing out of your cramped little stone crypt."

"Bah! Run along now little kitty, and take your friends with you."

Tellerick firmly pulled at her now. "Come on Kralla. We don't want anything to do with this."

They Have a History

Safely away from their close encounter with the Lord of Misery, Kralla finally managed to get a grip on her rage. Around her, the group had remained silent as they worked their way up the mountain.

"Master Tellerick," She growled. "Do you have any idea what happened back there?"

"What? Beyond us being used as bait to draw out Marakel? No, not really."

"It... Tamryn and Marakel knew each other?"

"They have a history. I know that much." Sighed Tellerick. "And it's a long one too. I really don't know the details Kralla. It's not something he ever talked about."

Acquaintances

Skaran put his hand to his head. "So... You know Master Tamryn as well Master Tellerick?"

"It's a little hard not to know about the order in these parts. And we may have gone on a few trips in the distant past."

"But when we went to see Master Tamryn..."

"We were always more acquaintances than friends Skaran. Like nodding to someone you see on the street regularly."

"Oh. And there I thought that you had some juicy tales to tell."

Kralla's ears twitched. "You already know far too much rat."

Skaran grinned. "You should know cat! Oh the tales..."

The Return of the Hat

The ground became difficult as they started to climb the mountain proper. Emerging from the mists that clung to the peaks above like a skirt, they were almost blinded by the brilliant sunshine. The air here was clear, crisp; a splash of ice-cold spring water to the face.

Kralla pulled her hat out of her pack and jammed it onto her head. Her cookie shaped ears poking through the bespoke covered holes.

"A flower for your hat dear lady?" Asked Skaran as he waved a daisy at her, grinning insanely.

"I'll flower you..." She growled back, baring a fang.

Daisy, Daisy...

Skaran, deftly sprang up, popped the daisy into Kralla's hat and barely managed to avoid her playful swipe on the way back down.

"Aww! Why so grumpy cat? If anyone should be feeling hard done by, it should be our boy Barnabas!"

"That's true rat." Kralla turned to the fox, while re-arranging the daisy to stay put. "Are you alright Barnabas?"

"Oh, I'm fine thanks. I'm not the first to be thrown beneath a cart by Master Tamryn. I'll wager I'll not be the last either! He's kind'a known for it. He's also known for taking care as well."

Looking Back

Kralla looked back down the trail. "Tamryn, and the Order, must have been trailing us since we left."

"Aye" nodded Skaran. "But he knew damn well that there were undead up here. He could've told us!"

"He used me as his bait. I shine brightly to the undead. He knew that I'd draw out whatever was controlling them. That's why he sent me with you." Sighed Barnabas. "He knew I'd be safe with you all."

"What's done is done. The cave of the Oracle is a little way above the snowline. We shall be there soon, hopefully." Said Master Tellerick.

Cold Weather Gear

The path turned to fine scree, making the footing treacherous, and finally to partially melted snow. The sun shone brightly above the clouds below them as the path moved from rock and ice to proper snow.

They stopped briefly to allow William and Master Tellerick to put on warmer clothes for the final climb.

Skaran stood to one side, looking pensively at his personal pack. What looked like a woollen scarf was visible where he'd partially pulled it from the pack. Sighing heavily he took it out, along with a pair of gloves and put them on. "OK, I know..."

Tail guard

Kralla snorted the water she was drinking from a flask when she turned and saw Skaran standing defeated and forlorn. "Let's get it over with..." He said. "I promised my old mum that I'd wear it if I went out in the cold. And let's face it, it's going to get cold."

Barnabas smiled. "That's erm, that's... Well. You don't see one of those every day. How do you, er, keep it on?"

"It's got some buttons that attach to my coat." He pulled at the woollen tail guard covering his tail.

"Well. It'll certainly keep it warm." Smiled Tellerick.

There's something magical...

Barnabas brought his own, ragged, brush around. "Maybe I should get one?" He smiled. "At least my fur is beginning to grow back now. Which reminds me!" He started rummaging in his pack, finally bringing out a small silver compact. He opened it and started applying the thick cream to the more naked parts of his tail.

Skaran clasped two paws over his nose. "Good goddess! What in hells name is in that?"

"I don't know. I daren't ask in case I find out. I do know is that it's working really well. I think there's something magical in it?"

I think we're alone now...

Kralla stood, hefting her pack onto her back. "Come on all. Let's get this over and done with. Then we can go home. The taste of my last beer is beginning to fade from my memory." She looked up along the snow-covered path. "Thank goodness the undead avoid the cold. It slows them down something terrible. So we should be... " As she spoke the word 'Alone' an enormous gout of flame erupted from the peak above them.

Alongside them, across from the path, the snow started moving as a single, monstrous, entity.

"Avalanche!" Shouted Skaran and Barnabas simultaneously.

A Wing and a Prayer

They watched as the mountainside appeared to slip, as a single piece, down into the valley below. It disappeared in a cloud of gritty snow that coated everything around them.

After the bone-shaking noise had died down, they looked up the path. Above them, where the path vanished into a small plateau marking the cave, there was the briefest glimpse of a tail and a wing.

"Was that a?" Shouted Barnabas, the roar of the mountain still ringing in his ears.

"Aye! I think it was!" Came the equally loud reply from Skaran.

"I hope not." Grumbled Master Tellerick.

There's a lot of it about...

An enormous, black and purple, muzzle appeared over the edge of the plateau above. "Hello? Is everyone alright down there? Sorry, I have a case of the sniffl..." There was a sudden intake of breath, and the muzzle disappeared. The sounds of someone stifling a sneeze came down the path, followed by said sneeze and another gout of searing flame.

They all looked up at the top of the path.

"There seems to be a lot of colds going about." Said Kralla.

"Aye. Was that a females voice I heard?"

Master Tellerick started forward. "Only one way to find out."

Amethyst

Finally, they climbed onto the small plateau leading to the cave entrance of the Oracle. The entrance itself appeared to be a relatively small affair, consisting of a deeply black entrance and a well-trodden path leading in. Sitting just outside the unadorned entrance sat the dragon.

It sniffed.

"Sorry about the avalanche. No one was caught in it were they?"

"No madam." Said Tellerick, stepping forwards. "Fortunately the path was clear of the snow."

The baleful yellow eyes followed the others as they climbed onto the flat space. "Hello there. My name is Amethyst." She sneezed, blasting fire again.

Bless You!

"Bless you!" Shouted Barnabas over the thunderous roar of flame.

Amethyst sniffed again, and wiped her nose. "Thank you sir. You wouldn't happen to be popping in to see the Oracle would you?"

"We are madam. May we assume that we can be of service?" Said Tellerick.

"Oh! Would you? So many thanks." She pulled at a set of scales on her chest, opening them like a purse. "Now... Where's that piece of paper?" She sniffed loudly again, before pulling out a large sheet. "I have a recipe, but I thought the Oracle might know where to find the ingredients?"

Ooh... That's a lot of honey...

Tellerick took the proffered paper from the dragons' claws as she delicately handed it to him.

He quickly glanced over it. "I might be able to help you with some of these actually."

"Really?" Said Amethyst. Trying to stifle a cough.

"Well, our village pub makes a very fine whiskey. I think they have a few casks stored away. It's a lot of honey though. That would be a trip into the city market for that, and I doubt that they would appreciate a dragon turning up on their doorstep. I'm sure that we could mediate for your gracious self?"

Why don't you just...

"Madam Amethyst, can't dragons use transformation magic? Surely you could simply see the Oracle yourself?" Asked Barnabas, making sure that master Tellerick was in front, alongside Kralla.

Amethyst tried to stifle another sneeze, but this time there was simply a huge cloud of black smoke that was whipped away by the wind. "No! My fire has gone out!" She wailed, before collapsing into a fit of coughing accompanied by more smoke. Finally managing to stop, she turned to face Barnabas. "It's a little difficult to do powerful magic, such as that when you are coughing and sneezing everywhere little fox."

We all have one...

William peered out from behind Barnabas at the enormous Dragon. Amethyst squinted at him. "And now I am intrigued." She looked straight at Master Tellerick. "You are here because of the little one Master Tellerick?"

"Aye madam, we are. He is a natural magic-user."

Amethyst sat up. "Come out little one. Let me get a better look at you." William held tightly onto Barnabas. She leaned forward once more. "Now where is your aura child?"

Now it was Tellerick's turn to frown. "Can you see something madam?"

She looked quizzically at William once more. "The boy's aura is missing."

An Aura Reading.

"You have me at a loss Madam. Will's aura is missing?" Tellerick looked at Will.

"Yes! Yours is a deep violet master Tellerick. You are filled with intuition. The universe flows through you"

Amethyst pointed at Skaran. "Yours, master Skaran, is a very pure yellow. You enjoy your fun, and hide your intellect behind it."

Then she moved on. "You, master Barnabas, you are blue. As suits your chosen path, you are filled with peace and truth amongst others."

"Whereas you, Mistress Kralla, you are a deep red. You are grounded, and stable yet able to be spontaneous when needed."

Interesting Times Ahead

Amethyst shook her head, and turned away, sneezing again she emitted another cloud of greasy black smoke. "Sorry." She sniffed.

"The boy has no aura, he just 'is' if you understand my meaning. I'm truly at a loss, and would very much like to hear what the oracle has to say about him." She wiped her nose. "Intrigued, indeed. There may be interesting times ahead. Hmm?" She blew her nose loudly into the giant handkerchief she had brought out. "I'd be more interested in my ingredients first though. I think I'm running a temperature, and that's never a good thing!"

A Warm Welcome

It felt warmer inside the cave than without. Before them the entrance constricted quickly down to a narrow fissure in the rock. The floor was clean, recently brushed and very well worn.

"Well Master Tellerick, this is your show now. We've done our part and delivered you to your destination. Do you want us to wait here, or shall we follow?" Kralla sniffed at the warm, dry air coming from the fissure.

"No wonder Amethyst couldn't get in here." Said Skaran as he dumped his pack onto the ground. Removing his coat and gloves, then stuffing them into the pack.

Warm Breeze

Along the worn walls of the fissure came a warm smell of cloves and other spices on a warm breeze that flowed outwards.

"Smells like mid-winters feast in here!" Sniggered Skaran. "Better than the usual mouldy old smell."

The fissure widened out into a large cavern. Scattered around the entrance were a few small tents, their occupants the source of the smells.

At the far end of the cavern, glowing softly was the aspect of the Oracle. Faintly visible in the dim light were crystal-like lines in the air, converging on the flat surface of the purple polygon.

The Oracle Speaks

Skaran nudged Barnabas as they walked towards the Aspect. "Is it my imagination, or does that look like a Chabbarat gambling dice?" Barnabas looked down at his companion.

"You mean die. Dice is more than one."

"Yeah, yeah. I know the singular, but no-one uses it. I'm not imagining it though am I?"

"No Skaran. You're not. it does look like one, except it's the size of a melon and glowing purple."

"Wonder why that is."

"IT IS BECAUSE I AM THE CONVERGENCE POINT OF TWENTY UNIVERSES RAT CALLED SKARAN." Before them, the ghostly image of a woman appeared.

It can be whatever it wants to be

Kralla raised her eyebrows. "It's a woman?!"

Tellerick patted her arm. "It can be whatever it wants to be." He stepped forward. "Oracle, I have brought someone for your opinion."

"REALLY HUMAN TELLERICK? AN OPINION? THAT IS NOT LIKE YOU."

Barnabas and Skaran sniggered at the back. "Girl's got sass." Said Skaran.

Tellerick gestured to William, as the image knelt on the worn stone floor becoming more solid as it did so. She beckoned.

"Come, young William." She held out her hand, her voice now less booming and coming from the Oracle herself instead of the air surrounding the group.

The Time has come again...

William knelt in front of the oracle, who sighed heavily. "That time has come again." She looked up at Tellerick. "You have brought the Augury before me because you do not recognise him."

It was Barnabas' turn to raise an eyebrow. "Wait, I know that..." He frowned, trying to remember where he'd seen the name before. "Augury..." If he had been human he would have paled, instead, the fur on the back of his neck bristled and stood on-end. "The sundering of the species. The Augury was the one who predicted the war of all ages, observing the birds."

A Sign of Change

"War?" Said Skaran and Kralla at the same time.

The Oracle stood. "The Augury is not a precursor of war, but of great changes in your world." She looked at Tellerick. "Change is inevitable Master Tellerick. The augury you have brought before me is young. He does not yet understand his role in your future events."

Tellerick bowed his head. "But you do. Don't you."

"And you know that I cannot tell you, even though I am considered an Oracle by your world. The appearance of the Augury is a sign of great change. Change that is fluid in time."

No Fate, But What You Make

"But, but you're the Oracle! You tell futures and things!" Spluttered Skaran.

She smiled. "Time is full of eddies, ripples and currents. It is not immutable, it is as water in a river. The appearance of the Augury blinds me." She looked back at William. "Your fate is what you make of it. Follow the teachings of Master Tellerick. Listen closely to the whispers of Amethyst, and be patient with Master Barnabas." He nodded. "Good. Trust your friends William. They will always be there for you." She stepped back. "I also believe Mistress Amethyst needs her shopping list filled out?"

Truth in the flight of birds

As they left the Oracle behind them, Will pulled on Tellericks' robe. "Master? What's an Augury?"

Tellerick smiled. "Most people would say that it is a tool for poking holes in things. But there's an obscure meaning that reaches far back into the past. I'm reasonably sure the Oracle means that one, and not the tool reference." He stopped, turned and knelt in front of William.

"An Augury is a person who can tell the future from the flights of the birds in the sky. And they are, very, special people indeed."

"And I am an Augury?"

"Yes. You are."

Ignore nothing

William looked at the ground. "I don't know how to do that."

Tellerick smiled. "And I do not have a clue how to teach you about prognostication either! I'm hoping that there is someone close by who will be able to though. I will carry on teaching you the basics; the standard magic's. But nothing the Oracle says should be taken lightly. Do you remember what she said about the whispers of Amethyst?" Will nodded. "I think that she meant our dragon friend outside. So we should hurry out and give Madam Amethyst her shopping list back don't you think?"

Don't go back the way you came...

Outside, the dragon was hanging its head over the side of the plateau.

"Ahem! Madam? We have your list!" Said Tellerick loudly. The dragons head rose up from below, and Amethyst wiped her mouth.

"Sorry." She looked down over the edge, then quickly looked away. "Erm, I'm afraid I've been a bit ill. You shouldn't go back the way you came." She reached out and took the list, reading it quickly. "Hmm... You said you could help with some of these?"

"Madam, I'm sure we can."

"Then I shall give you a lift down the mountain as payment. Hop on!"

Back down the mountain...

A few hours later Amethyst settled onto the ground next to the monastery, where Barnabas had to quickly run to and tell them not to gather weapons.

"Blimey. Weeks of trekkin' over in a blink." Said Skaran. "You should do a taxi service missy. Earn a fortune!"

Amethyst blew her nose messily. "I'm not a taxi. That was..." She sneezed into the sky, emitting an enormous gout of blue flame. "Bleurgh! That was payment, rat. And you need to lose weight!"

Skaran looked down and patted his paunch. "I'm no dwarf missy dragon, but I can quaff with the best!"

Smoke and Fire

Amethyst sat on her rump and wiped her nose yet again. "So, master Tellerick, before I lose my voice. What did the Oracle have to say for herself?"

"Well mistress Amethyst, the Oracle said that Will is the Augury."

Amethyst burst into a fit of coughing and sneezing, emitting fire and smoke that lit the late afternoon sky and blanketed the ground in foul-smelling soot; forcing everyone to rush to the monastery for cover.

Managing to calm down, the dragon signalled it was safe for Tellerick to approach. "He's the Augury? Oh, bloody hellfire. That's not good." She croaked.

First Responder

"Why is that not good? Beyond what the Oracle told us about the last time the Augury appeared."

Amethyst sighed heavily, then coughed again. "Because as the first dragon to meet the Augury, I now have to attend him." She thumped the ground. "Hell and damnation! Why couldn't it have been Audrey? She loves this kind of thing! Bloody cold." She grumbled.

"So you will be staying with us?"

Amethyst rolled her eyes. "Yes. But don't expect me to pull your bony arses out of the fire when it comes to it. I'm here for the boy alright?"

"Fair enough"

A bed innkeep!

Amethyst looked around. "Nice enough place you have here fox. Any chance of a barn I can sleep in?"

Barnabas whispered in the ear of an increasingly horrified monk. "There is a stone annex that's used for wintering the animals. Will that be alright?"

"So long as it's clean, that'll do. I'll do my own bedding." She looked down at Will. "That's lesson number one boy. If you have trouble sleeping, bring your own pillow." She winked at him. "And you, tiger."

"That's Kralla thank you."

Amethyst reached into her pouch and pulled out a handful of gems. "Your retainer."

A retainer for services rendered.

Kralla looked at her cupped paws full of large gems. A couple of rubies, three diamonds, emeralds, sapphires. Amethyst leaned in closely.

"Don't get any ideas. I ain't made of money tigress. But the boy is under my wing now and he needs a good set of claws by his side. I know a pro when I see one princess, even if she is dossing about in the low lands."

At the sound of the word *princess*, Kralla's pupils widened and she looked sharply at the dragon. Again, Amethyst winked. This time knowingly, before turning away and sneezing once again.

Where's my room?

Amethyst got up and leaned over the monk standing next to Barnabas. "Right then! Where's my room?" The monk looked along Amethyst's muzzle and into her eyes, terror gripping his insides.

"Th... Thi..."

"Spit it out, man!"

The monk started to shake uncontrollably as Barnabas bowed. "Allow me to show you Mistress Amethyst." He nodded at the monk, and then in the direction of the monastery. The monk bowed and then streaked across the grounds and through the giant doors to illusory safety.

Amethyst ambled behind Barnabas. "You have a nice place here fox."

"Thank you mistress Amethyst. Greatly appreciated."

How did we end up with a dragon?

As Amethyst disappeared behind the monastery, Kralla turned to Tellerick. "How in the Goddesses name did we end up with a dragon?"

"It seems that the fates have conspired to keep us moving along this path. I know that Will here is simply standing in the eye of the storm, everything swirling around him..."

Skaran sat down on his pack. "So, are you saying that staying close to your boy is the safest place to be Master Tellerick?"

Tellerick sighed heavily. "Will is the Augury. Great change is coming, and often that leads to great strife. War might be inevitable."

She pays well

Kralla pinched the bridge of her nose tightly and sighed herself. "I wasn't planning on sticking around after we returned Master Tellerick. I was on my way to the Clarrianne Plateau. I only took your job because I needed a little extra cash."

"Madam Whitesnow. I think that the Oracle has dented all our plans."

"You can say that again Master Tellerick." Said Skaran. "Although, you have to admit Kralla. The old bat does pay well."

Kralla picked a ruby and eyed it. "That she does Skaran." And tossed it over to the rat.

"Bloody hell that's a nice gem."

Fates entwined

Skaran tossed the giant ruby back to Kralla. "Missy, I may be a pack-rat, but I have a family. The old bat paid you, not me."

Tellerick and Kralla looked at one another and laughed in unison. "Wot?" Said Skaran.

"You're as wrapped up in this as the rest of us Rat!" Growled Kralla mirthfully. "You really think that you're not bound to young Will?" She laughed again. "Tell him Master Tellerick."

"She's right Skaran. We were bound together by the Oracle from the moment we entered the cave. Our fates entwined, by our world itself!"

"Gaagh!" Groaned Skaran.

Where's he off to?

As Skaran fell over backwards, bemoaning his fate, a horse bolted past. On its back the terrified monk from before. Skaran pushed himself up onto his elbows. "Now where is he buggering off to I wonder?"

The others watched as the horse, and rider, disappeared into the distance...

Barnabas watched Amethyst as she brushed the floor with her tail. Huge plumes of dust, and old bedding, flew out of the huge doors to the stone barn.

"Shoo fox. Stand outside and wait. I need to set my bed." Forewarned he left quickly, followed by the sound of metal on stone.

Bed Linen

"Alright!" Bellowed Amethyst from within the barn. Barnabas peered around the door, his mind boggled as he did-so. The stone floor was layered, at least two feet deep, with gold coins.

"I don't see any precious gems." He said quietly.

"I like a soft bed. None of those silly stones that some dragons like. Also no pots, pans or other large items. They're lumpy as anything."

"I've never seen so much..."

"Don't be getting any ideas." She pointed to the edge of the pile. "Take one outside."

Barnabas took a coin through the door. It quickly turned to stone.

A message to town

Barnabas looked back at Amethyst. "Now that is a neat trick. How many people have you caught out with that?"

"Far too many." She said, smugly. "Now go away, I've got a headache and I'm knackered."

Barnabas nodded and pushed the barn door closed.

On his way back to the others, a small mouse in a monks habit tugged at his coat.

"Master Barnabas? Please, wait a moment?"

"What is it, brother?"

"Master Barnabas, the abbot has sent word to the dragon slayers guild about the... er... dragon."

"He's done what!?"

"He sent brother Carmichael to town on the horse."

Slish... Slish...

Kralla looked up from her sword, the whetstone halfway along its length. "Why are you huffing and puffing Fox?"

Barnabas took a moment to catch his breath.

"The abbot has sent a message to the dragon slayer guild about Amethyst."

Skaran's head snapped round. "He what!?"

Barnabas looked around, confused. "Where is master Tellerick and William?"

Kralla's whetstone slished the rest of the way down the shining blade, making it ring. "He went on ahead to take the boy home. The only people who know he's the augury are us and the dragon. Security in obscurity master Tellerick called it."

Let the Dragon take care of it!

"So what do we do?" Huffed Barnabas.

"Let the dragon take care of it." Kralla started polishing the blade on her lap.

"But... The dragon slayers guild!"

Kralla looked up. "Barnabas. If you hadn't noticed, she is an old dragon."

"Then we must do something!"

Kralla laughed out loud. "Fox, you betray your naivety. Ask yourself the question. How is Amethyst such an old dragon?"

Barnabas gave her a bemused look. "Because she's avoided the dragon slayers?"

"No. It's because she's probably one of the most feared dragons in this world. Experience, knowledge and likely the wiles to use them."

Sit down Fox

Kralla went back to sharpening her sword, as Skaran went over to Barnabas and patted him on the chest. "Sit down fox, relax. We're going to need to be able to move around quickly when the show starts."

"Show?"

"Yeah! Should be a good one too. Old scaly looks like she's got the nadgers to take care of a slayer quickly, but it still might get a little toasty."

Barnabas looked down at the rat. "Have you seen a dragon battle then?"

Skaran laughed out loud. "O'Course not! I should imagine not many have and lived to tell the tale!"

Help the monks pack

Barnabas sat down on the far end of the log Kralla was sitting on. "Do you really think that we should just stand by?"

Kralla huffed. "We'd only get in the way. If you really want to do something useful you'd better go help the monks pack up." She pointed at the side of the monastery where some horses and pack lizards were being gathered. "That idiot abbot of yours brought this on himself and your brethren. The least you could do is rub it in his nose. I can't wait till Tamryn gets back. He's gonna be so pissed!"

Baked ruins

Barnabas got up and started walking back towards the monastery.

"Oh!" Shouted Skaran after him. "If they're not taking it with them, can you check to see if they've got any loo roll and soap they don't mind letting us have? We're running low and things are gonna get real smoky and ashy round here soon."

Barnabas rolled his eyes, and shouted back over his shoulder. "I'll ask!"

Skaran sniggered and Kralla glanced across at him. "What's amused you rat?"

"Heh, just thinkin' about what you said about what master Tamryn's gonna say when he gets back to baked ruins."

Fast or slow?

"I suspect you might very well learn some new swear words rat."

"Oh, I don't know about that missy." He grinned. "But maybe I can loan master Tamryn some new ones!"

"So... If you were a betting rat... Fast or slow?"

Skaran scratched his chin and looked thoughtful. "Dunno. I'm all for the big showy stuff, but she's a wily old lizard. She won't let'im go, that's fer certain. He'd likely bring back reinforcements..."

Kralla nodded.

"... I think there'll be a bit o'bluster, a big flash'n it'll be all over in a few seconds."

"So quick then?"

Skaran nodded.

A few more seconds then?

"I'll give the slayer a few more seconds than that. They do have flame-proof armour, and the guild's tactics are renowned. But like you said, Amethyst is a wily old lady. I don't know. She might just blast him into ash the moment he goes through the door." Said Kralla thoughtfully.

"She's not very well though. There might be a lot o'smoke and no fire."

Kralla put down her sword and slid it into its sheath. "Good point. She's not well." Kralla pulled her other sword from its sheath and started sharpening it. "We might have to step in."

Eww!

"She could always throw-up on him."

Kralla looked sharply at Skaran and they both shuddered simultaneously.

"Aye. Maybe not. That would not be a nice way to go."

"Skaran, keep thoughts like that to yourself please. Lest I have to tie your mouth shut."

"Sorry big cat. My mouth gets away from me sometimes."

"Hmmm... I had noticed." She smirked, and then looked across to Barnabas helping the monks load the animals. "I think we might have to hold Barnabas back initially. He's likely to get himself hurt if we don't."

"Aye lass. I've got rope at the ready."

A call for a Slayer

"Sir Albrecht! Sire! A message from the Order!"

Albrecht rolled his eyes and sighed. He put down the polishing cloth and the pauldron he'd been working on.

"What is it now, boy?" He lifted a nearby goblet of wine.

"A dragon! A dragon has roosted in a monastery in the foothills. A messenger from the Order of Masterful Sepulchre arrived this morning."

Albrecht rolled his eyes again. "Probably another lizard and not a dragon."

"The messenger described it. Huge he said, black as night with enormous purple wings."

Wine sprayed across the boys face as Albrecht coughed and spluttered loudly.

Mother of Dragons

Albrecht wiped his greying beard on his sleeve. "Gods dammit! The Mother of Dragons!" He coughed again. "Boy. Prepare our gear, we must leave as soon as possible."

"Sire? The 'Mother of Dragons'?"

"I recognise the description. This is an elder dragon that the guild has been trying to slay for centuries. It is a duty reserved for the experienced members of the guild."

"Like yourself sire?"

"Aye lad. Now run along and prepare. We must move quickly. This one is rarely down from its mountain in the North. Although I must wonder, boy, why is it so far south?"

Let them know...

Albrecht mounted his horse. Behind them, a mule carried his plate armour and other gear. His page boy mounted his pony and brought it alongside Sir Albrecht's massive shire horse. He beckoned to the boy.

"Boy. You cannot come with me."

"But sire! I must!"

"Not this one Fred." He patted the boy's shoulder. "This one is a wily beast, and very old. It's bested so many before me, and I won't underestimate it. The last thing I want is for you to get in the way."

"Sire... I..."

"I want you to return to the guild. Let them know."

Dinner break

Kralla waved from the bench, a leg of turkey in her other hand as Tellerick came around the bend in the road.

"Hail!" She shouted, before turning to Skaran. "Best go get Barnabas."

"He was headed for more wine, so he's probably in the cellar." Skaran got up from the bench and headed towards the main building.

Tellerick approached the table and sat down. "And how is everyone?"

"Well as can be. The dragon still has her cold. You should hear her snoring at night!" Kralla rolled her eyes. "We set up camp over towards the woods, she is... loud."

There's a problem brewing

Tellerick sat down; and grabbing a plate, started to fill it with food from the table.

"William isn't with you Master Tellerick?" Asked Kralla.

"No. I thought it best to leave him with his father. He needs his family right now more than he needs us. He needs to be grounded by them."

"He has a lot of power, doesn't he."

Tellerick nodded. "I understand now why we've been drafted by fate to be at his side. He has yet to come into his own. We need to prepare him for whatever is coming..."

"About that... There's a problem brewing..."

Stumbling from one disaster to another

Tellerick sighed. "It's like we're just stumbling from one disaster to another. What is it now?"

"The Abbot sent for a dragon slayer to kill Amethyst. I believe that there may be one in town." Kralla growled, before taking a bite out of the Turkey leg she was holding. Most of it disappeared.

"Well it's only a day's ride from here. When did the messenger leave?"

"Not long after you did."

"That means he'll be here soon."

"I know. Barnabas wants to fight them. I've said no, let the dragon deal with them."

"She's an old dragon. You're probably right."

Guild reputations

"What do you mean? She's probably right?!" Asked Barnabas as he approached the table holding a pitcher of wine. Tellerick turned to him.

"Barnabas, sit down. I think that we need to have a chat."

"What? About someone coming here with the express purpose of slaying Amethyst? Don't be ridiculous! We have to stop them!" He slammed the pitcher down on the table, wine sloshed violently inside.

"Barnabas, Amethyst is an old dragon!"

"And?"

Tellerick sighed heavily. "She old because she's probably seen most of the slayer guild die. They're not just known for their victories, but their mortality rate!"

Watch a pro

"Achoo!" Suddenly the table was engulfed in thick, black, smoke. "Sorry!" Rumbled Amethyst, before coughing some more and sniffing loudly.

The others coughed and looked up.

"So... That idiot of an Abbot sent for a dragon slayer. I'm trying not to laugh because my chest is aching like buggery." Amethyst sniggered loudly.

"Aren't you worried?!"

Amethyst looked weary. "Nope. I've been dealing with these guys for centuries. Got a, er, little trick for dealing with them." She winked at Barnabas.

"Trick? They're dragon slayers! We can stop them before they get to you!"

"Fox. Stay put. And watch a pro."

Don't interfere fox

"When he arrives, send him in. I'm not going anywhere anytime soon." Amethyst turned to go.

"Oh, I organised the things on your list by the way." Piped Tellerick. "There'll be some barrels arriving the day after tomorrow."

"Many thanks Master Tellerick. My cold won't appreciate it, but I certainly will." She looked over her shoulder at Barnabas. "Don't interfere fox. I mean it! I've got this covered. If you want to do something, kindly ask the Abbot not to do it again or there will be consequences. Understood?"

Barnabas nodded. "I'll have a talk with him about it shortly."

Resplendent

They heard the clank of full plate on horseback before they saw the dragon slayer. Albrecht came around the corner and into full view; resplendent in his polished and dragon-fire proof armour.

"Where is the dragon!?" He bellowed.

Kralla put a firm paw on Barnabas's shoulder as he started snarling. "Don't make me do something you'll regret Barnabas. Amethyst is ready for him remember."

"Doesn't mean I have to like it." He growled under his breath.

"I don't either, but you'd best heed the warning of a dragon."

Tellerick got up from the table and pointed to the barn.

Come out Dragon!

"Come out Dragon!" Shouted Albrecht. He, and his horse, stood outside the barn door.

"You can come in!" Replied Amethyst, loudly.

Albrecht paused. It hadn't been the response he usually got from a dragon. So this was it. He looked around and sighed, lowering his sword. Behind him, someway up the hill towards the forest, the others watched expectantly. At least he had an audience.

"Can I bring my horse?"

"Of course you can!" She said, a little lower this time. "Get your aging fat butt in here Albrecht. There's no need to make a scene out there. Tch! Honestly!"

"Retirement" Plans

Albrecht dismounted and led his horse inside the barn.

"The lady Amethyst I believe. It is a pleasure to meet you."

"Hrmph!" Amethyst rolled her eyes. "So... You are aware of the retirement plan?"

"Yes milady. It is a closely guarded secret within the guild's senior slayers."

"Damn right it needs to be a secret. Can't go around letting the management know I've been skimming the cream off the top of their precious slayers."

"Do we need to make a scene Ma'am? There are people outside."

"No. They're fine. They'll need to know at sometime. Might as well be now."

Pastry Chef

"So, Albrecht. I hear you make a mean pastry." Amethyst smacked her lips.

"Patisserie Ma'am."

"Ooh. I always enjoy a good sweet. We should be able to accommodate your talent for baking."

She rose and towered over Albrecht. "Fortunately, this is a wand spell. I have a cold if you hadn't noticed." She rummaged around in a pocket and brought out a gnarly stick before drawing a door on the wall of the barn. "Give the others a shout, would you?" She coughed, and then sneezed blowing the end off of the barn in a giant gout of blue fire.

Dust and debris

Albrecht's horse galloped, screeching, at full speed out of the black cloud. Dust, debris and huge chunks of masonry rained down in the field. The barns' cornerstone landed with a wet thud, throwing up dirt and clods of grass.

Albrecht staggered from the cloud, covered in a layer of thick black dust. Coughing, he managed to open his eyes as Barnabas's fist met his jaw with everything the fox had. Albrecht span, and landed heavily on the floor.

"St.. stop! I... " He cried, pushing himself up, as the giant black silhouette of Amethyst rose up. Coughing and spluttering herself.

Friend or Foe

"DROP HIM NOW!" Roared Amethyst. Her huge wings outstretched blacked out the sun behind her as she towered over the remains of the barn.

Barnabas's Jaw dropped, as the enormity of having a dragon close by rammed itself home. Amethyst had shifted from friend to dangerous entity in a matter of seconds. It was something none of them were prepared for. Friend or foe, Amethyst was a force to be reckoned with.

Suddenly his mouth was clamped shut by a huge white paw as Kralla's arm wrapped around his chest and he was hoisted into the air by the tigress.

Whoopsie!

"Oh... No... Shouldn't have done that!" Amethyst's eyes rolled up, her wings pulled in and she collapsed onto the ruined masonry of the barn beneath her.

"Sir Albrecht! Sir Albrecht! You have slain the dragon! Oh, praises be!" Came a shout from behind the short-wall bordering the monastery. Albrecht looked round, as did Kralla, Tellerick and Skaran. Barnabas struggled uselessly in the tigresses vice-like grip, huffing loudy through his nose as he struggled to breath.

"Boy! No! What have you done? I told you to return to the guild. You cannot follow me to where I am going!"

The 'Arrangement'

Albrecht's page boy vaulted the short wall and ran to him. "Sire, please, let me help you."

Albrecht stood and wiped the blood from his face, before sighing heavily. "Boy, you will have to come with me now."

Everyone looked quizzically at Albrecht. "Sire?"

"I did not come here to slay the Dragon. I came here to retire."

"Sire? I. I don't understand! Did you mean to let the Dragon kill you?"

"Hah!" Bellowed Albrecht. "No. There is an 'arrangement' that the elder slayers have with this Dragon."

Behind him there was a groan, followed by the scraping of masonry.

A decent right hook

Amethyst rolled over and vomited noisily into an empty sheep pen, before slowly sitting up.

The eyes of Albrecht's page widened in terror as Amethyst brought her head around to scowl at the group.

"What's going on?" She squinted at Barnabas. "I told you to stay out of this fox. It's my business."

Barnabas's ears flattened and he hung limp in Kralla's vice-like grip as Albrecht stood between them. "Please Ma'am. His intentions were obviously noble. Plus he has a fairly decent right hook." He sniffed. "Nearly broke my nose!" He turned to Kralla. "Put him down madam Tigress."

A Gateway

Kralla gently put Barnabas down, where he promptly collapsed to the floor gasping for air. "What, exactly, is going on here Amethyst?" She asked.

"It's probably better that I show you, than try and explain." She started rummaging in the rubble. "Ah! There you are!" She pulled a worn looking branch of a tree from beneath the remains of the barn.

"A wand?"

"Yes Master Tellerick. It's a gateway wand." She stood, a little unsteadily, and proceeded to draw a door on the side of the nearby chapel, before tapping lightly at the four corners and bringing it to life.

Sea Air

In a blaze of light, they were suddenly engulfed in an offshore wind. The sweet smell of the ocean flooded out of the new gateway.

"Come along. And don't forget your page Albrecht. He was your charge before, but now your responsibility for him is profoundly serious. This is a secret that has been kept for generations of slayers over a thousand years."

She turned to the others. "Don't discuss this with anyone on pain of a brief, but very fiery, death." They all nodded.

"Good. Please go through. It will be nice to get some sea air for'a bit."

Welcome to Hoardmouthe

In the distance a small town snuggled down into a bay that formed a natural harbour. The hills dipped down towards the town, but also rose towards the sea forming tall cliffs that looked out over a cerulean blue ocean. On one end an imposing tower stood, its top clad in glass.

Amethyst cleared her throat and made a face before coughing again and spouting black smoke. "Welcome..." She said, wheezing. "To Hoardmouthe."

Tellerick looked down on the village. "Hoardmouthe? This isn't where you keep your hoard is it?!"

Amethyst nodded. "Don't go spreading it around alright? It's a secret."

Hail!

A horse approached on the path to the village.

"Hail! Hail Dragon Amethyst!" Shouted the bearded man.

"I try and keep it informal around here." She winked.

"It is good to see you again Mistress of the Magma."

"And you too Siegmund. We have a new resident to our town. Do please ensure he has lodgings on the Bakers street."

Siegmund dismounted and looked at the others. "Ma'am?"

"Oh, these are just visitors." She sniffed and wiped her nose.

"You still have your cold Mistress?"

"Yes!" She grumbled. "If only the brewery could produce a half decent Whiskey." She sighed.

A Distiller of Renown

"I might have a suggestion there Dragon... Come here boy and stop cowering, this one's not going to kill you." Albrecht pulled his squire up. "Stand straight." Trying to control his terror, the page boy stood bolt straight as if he'd been turned to stone where he stood. "Gagh!" Exclaimed the slayer. "This one's father is a spirits smith. A distiller of renown, and terrible father having placed his boy in the guild."

Amethyst eyed the boy. "Is this true?"

He nodded. She sniffed. "We have a distiller amongst us! Well done Albrecht. Now I won't have to eat him."

Matchstick Tower

As Amethyst finished her announcement, the boy collapsed like a matchstick tower into a pile of youthful, spindly, arms and legs.

"Well, he certainly had the fear of dragons put in him." Master Tellerick looked on as Albrecht picked up the boy.

"Some are meant to be slayers, and some are not." Replied Albrecht. "This one was not. His father had ideas above his station involving nobility; and sending his son to the guild was his way of getting on the ladder... So-to-speak." Albrecht looked down. "But he's a good lad, with a big heart. He'll learn quickly."

Training?

Amethyst turned to the newcomer. "So... News mister Donner?"

"Nothing of muchness mistress dragon. Another pirate raid this last week, taken care of by the children. All were dispatched and their ship rendered into parts for the fishing fleet. That one was good for the town coffers."

Kralla, Telleric, Barnabas and Skaran looked at him. "Er, the litt'le kiddies took down a ship full of pirates?" Frowned Skaran.

"Aye! 'Tis a fun part of their training as dragon slayers mister rat."

"Trainin'? I'm er, gettin' real confused now. Don't missy dragon-draws ere get the gold from the ship then?"

The Nature of the Hoard

Donner scratched his beard; it was his turn to frown. "And what would Mistress Amethyst want with all those gold coins and jewels and things?"

Skaran turned to Amethyst. "Don't you use these guys to collect your hoard of gold stuff together then missy?"

Amethyst laughed out loud before collapsing into a cloud of hissing black smoke. She took a moment to compose herself. "Oh my Goddess! You think I hoard golden trinkets?"

"Ain't that what all dragons hoard?"

"Oh mister Skaran. You absolute dear! That's like humans hoarding mattresses and pillows! I don't hoard gold! I hoard Dragon Slayers!"

A Highly Regarded Service

Skaran's jaw dropped open. "You wot?" Everyone else looked at Amethyst aghast.

"I hoard Dragon Slayers." She said with a smile. "All the best come from here and retire here. Occasionally we get new blood." She waved at Sir Albrecht. "But generally we supply the Dragon Slayers' guild with the best slayers around."

"But, but... Don't that mean you're killin' your own kin?" Skaran was very obviously struggling with the concept.

"When your kind step out of line, you reign them in, so do I. It's a highly regarded service within dragon social circles. My slayers are, basically, dragon police."

The Audacity

Skaran sat down with an audible thud. His tail straight out and a look of disbelief on his face, as the audacity of the whole thing sank in.

The dragon had infiltrated the dragon slayers guild completely, hoarded the best and even started supplying the guild with the most highly trained dragon slayers in the world. She'd then used those self-same dragon slayers as her personal police force to keep the other dragons in line.

It was... Spectacular. Not to mention, as an elder, the guild would only send her the best to slay her.

"Dammit Missy. You're good!"

An Apex Machiavellian Predator

Towering above them all the apex, Machiavellian, predator that was Amethyst looked smug. "Yes rat. Yes I am."

She looked down the towards the village as a small cart approached. On the back was a cage containing a man.

"What is this Siegmund?"

"Ah. The children captured a pirate. As you are here, I thought you would want to talk with him before he's put down."

"I'm tired Siegmund, and I have a raging headache. Why do I need to talk to a pirate of all people?"

"Well, this one is a little odd Ma'am."

"Really? How odd?"

"Very ma'am."

I Haven't Seen One Of These In AGES!

"Oh my! I haven't seen one of these in nearly a thousand years!"

As it approached the group, the man inside the cage hissed and clanked as he railed against the bars of his cage.

Amethyst sat down and peered through the bars as the cart stopped in front of them.

The man wasn't a man. Underneath the ragged clothes the skin hung loose, revealing filigree iron metalwork. Artisan nuts and rivets, over precision gears levers and hissing pipework.

It reached and scrabbled for the dragon, intent on getting to her but unable to understand the bars blocking its way.

And then it...

As the creature inside the cage started whistling like a kettle beginning to boil, Amethyst quickly placed one enormous paw underneath the cart and launched it out over the bay.

"Shield your eyes!" She shouted as she brought a wing around the group. There was a brilliant flash, so bright the individual bones in Amethysts' wing were clearly visible. Followed by a hot wind that picked up grass and dust from the ground.

Amethyst looked down on the stunned group. "Is everyone alright?"

Everyone in the crook of her wing blinked the dark spots and dust away from their eyes.

An Automaton

"Wot the bleedin' hell's teef was that!" Screeched Skaran, as the group picked themselves up from the ground.

"That, rat." Said Amethyst. "Was a dragon slaying automaton. They are skin wearers.

"Skin wearers?" An edge of terror skirted Barnabas's voice. "Really?"

"Yes, fox. The flesh of a person stitched over the cold skeleton of iron cogs and springs. Intricate in their monstrousness. They are magical constructs of incredible ingenuity and require knowledge, that I thought was out of reach for a good thousand years."

"That was quite the light show." Tellerick brushed himself down. "A lot of magic used there."

Automata Abroad

Amethyst brushed at her wing, dislodging dust and dead scales. "We should not dally here. With automata abroad in the world it is clear that change is on the horizon."

Tellerick looked back at the portal. "I should return to the boy. There are forces at play that none of us are truly prepared for."

"Especially Will." Replied Kralla. "He's a just child Tellerick. He shouldn't have to deal with all... All this!"

"The augury simply won't have to mistress Kralla." Said Amethyst gently. "That is what we are here for. That is why we are bound to his presence."

A Parting of the Ways

"This is where we part ways master Albrecht. I look forwards to visiting your shop in the near future."

"Mistress." Albrecht bowed deeply before Amethyst. "I thank you for honoring the agreement. Also, for not broiling my idiot page."

"Think nothing of it. Although I would remind him that revealing the secret of Hoardmouthe has a deliciously... crispy ending." To which the page visibly turned pale as the blood drained from his face.

Albrecht wrapped a thick, muscle-bound arm around the page's shoulders. "Come along boy. Let's get settled in for the night. There's lots of work needs doing!"

A Bellowing Return

As they passed through the portal, returning to the hallowed ground of the monastery the bellowing of an angry honey badger filled the air.

"Where the blazes have you been boy!" Tamryn stomped across the courtyard. "What in hells teeth happened to our barn?!" He stopped as Amethyst squeezed through. "What!" He yelled at the fox. "Are you doing with a bloody dragon?!"

Barnabas opened his mouth to start. "Oh shut up boy! We have a situation here!" He turned. "You and you." He pointed at two monks. "Flasks and Candles" He turned back to Barnabas. "The lich escaped us."

The Race to Misery

Tamryn continued to bark orders into the disarray until Tellerick placed his hand on Tamryn's shoulder. "What do you mean, the lich escaped you? Marakel?"

"Aye, Marakel. That smug, nasty un-life." Snarled Tamryn. "Gerald lost focus on him and fell asleep on the job, while that bundle of bones that calls itself a necromancer slid off into the night."

Tellerick paled and turned to Kralla. "Will." They said in Unison.

Skaran's jaw dropped open, "Oh shit..."

"He's at the woodcutter's on the edge of the old town Kralla." Said Tellerick. "Get to him quickly, I'll be right behind you!"

Running

Kralla sped off down the road. Right now, she needed strength when she got to the boy, so she quickly settled into a long loping run that her pride used when running down plains lizards. It conserved energy while still allowing a fair amount of speed. Of course, she was far faster than anyone at the monastery. Except maybe for the dragon as she could fly.

But the dragon didn't know where the boy lived. She did.

Pads and claws dug into the packed road dirt, kicking up little puffs of brown dust as she sped towards the woodcutters' house.

Scent of Decay

The small house of the woodcutter appeared cold and silent as Kralla came up the track. This was what she was born for. The hunt. Her nose flared, sampling the breeze. The boys scent was here, fresh; but mingled with the dust of ages. The musty smell of the tomb. Marakel, the lich, was here, somewhere.

Close.

Suddenly she span around, simultaneously unsheathing her swords with a loud metallic *slish*.

"Oh, ho! You are still a nimble little kitty aren't you!" Laughed Marakel behind her.

"Why don't you come here and find out bonesy. Taste the edge of my blades?"

Little Bunny

The monk ran across the courtyard with a large leather satchel and deposited it before Tamryn, before rushing off again. The old badger opened it to check its contents before looping it over his head. "Where's my horse!?" He bellowed before turning to Tellerick. "You think he's gone after your boy master Tellerick?"

"Aye. the woodcutter's boy. We need to get there quickly."

A shadow crossed the pair; Amethyst's head came close. "Point the way Master Tellerick." An enormous hand-paw grabbed him. "You too little bunny." As her other hand-paw engulfed Tamryn, cutting off his cry of indignation.

Play with the cat

The heavy sound of one of Kralla's blades embedding itself into the side of a tree rebounded across the small clearing in front of the woodcutters wooden cottage.

"Tamryn must've done a real number on you lich." She snarled. "You're slow."

"Oh! Come now! One should always play with one's pets dear kitty."

The wood splintered heavily with a crack as she twisted the blade from the tree. She sprang at Marakel, brandishing both blades. He fell backwards and feinted to one side as one of them narrowly missed his arm.

"No magic yet?" She hissed, as she lunged again.

Which way to the woodcutters again?

Amethyst launched into the sky, powerful wings beating down. The downdraft sending monks, foxes and rats scattering.

"Bloody hell missy!" Shouted Skaran from a pile of hay. "E're? Where's this woodcutter's shed then?"

Barnabas spat hay as he too crawled out from the stack. "Bleurgh! P'th, p'th! Not far, but it's going to be a bit of a run."

"Last one there gets to dig 'is bonieness's 'ole where we bury his skinny arse in the ground!" And with that, Skaran leapt out of the hay stack and streaked across the yard before stopping. "Er... Which way fox?" Barnabas pointed.

That way to the Woodcutters'

"Mmph! Mmmmfrah!" Amethyst realised that she was not only clenching her teeth, but also her fist. The one with the priest in it. She relaxed and Tamryn's head popped out between her claws, panting for air. "Hell's teeth dragon! Warnings! And if you call me a rabbit again...!"

"You'll do what exactly?" She said loudly over the beat of her wings. She looked down. There were numerous small clearings with cottages and other small-holdings scattered along the edge of the woods.

"There!" Shouted Tellerick. "Down there!" The flash of steel in sunlight told he where to go. She dove.

Gotcha

Marakel dodged again, but it was obvious now that he was struggling. The child was here, he could feel him close by but it was dull, covered.

Kralla struck out again, this time catching him with a leg as she pirouetted around her last sword thrust. Marakel careened across the clearing and struck one of the charcoal drums, tipping it over and spilling Will and his father into the fray. Instantly Marakel reached for the boy and drew him close.

"Ah, ah! Kitty... You don't want to hurt the boy do you?"

Kralla roared as she skidded to a stop.

Comparisons

A beat of distant wind caught Kralla's ear as they swivelled in irritation. She was hot; and now she was exceptionally angry at the Lich, Marakel, as he held young William close to his chest. She snarled and leaned as if to strike.

"Ah, ah, aaah! Don't think I won't!"

"You don't have the balls, Lich"

"Neither, fortunately, do you miss Kitty."

Kralla started prowling. She couldn't help it. Pacing back and forth as the Lich kept all his attention on her.

"Mine are considerably bigger than what's in your dried up sack."

"Oh, I absolutely don't doubt that cat!"

Handling Power

"So, what's the deal here bones?" Snarled Kralla as she paced back and forth. "You're drained of power and just need the boy as a hostage? A bit low for the so called lord of miserly."

"That's Lord of Misery dearest kitty cat. Originally it was that, but even I know real power when I handle it." The lich lifted young Will higher up the withered remains of his chest.

"Hah! The boy has no powers bones. He's just that. A boy."

"Oh no miss kitty. No, no, no." He cast his gaze downwards. "He's so much more than that!"

From Above

Kralla's huge paw-hands flashed as the Lich looked down on Will. Her knife flew between the space separating them in a single heartbeat, only to be caught and casually tossed back. It clattered across the stones on the path.

"Not bad kitty." Smirked Marakel. "Not bad. But you are still no match for me, even on a bad day."

"It must be a bad day then for you to need to hold a child between us. You sad old bag of bones. You can't even..."

Suddenly the space around them turned dark as Amethyst, roaring, plummeted from the sky."

Your Fate

Amethyst landed heavily behind Marakel. Her wings cupped around, plunged the tableau into darkness except for the infernal, purple glow coming from the dragons eyes and mouth. The clawed tips of her wings dug deep into the ground around them, ensuring no easy means of escape.

"LIIICH!" She hissed and drooled. The latter sending up acidic whisps of smoke as it burned into the ground.

Marakel span around, holding Will up as a shield. "He's mine dragon!"

"NO." Burbled Amethyst. "MY WORD IS MAGIC. I BIND YOU LICH. I BIND YOU TO THE BOY. YOUR FATE BELONGS TO HIM NOW."

What? What have you done!?

"What? What have you done!" Marakel dropped Will to the floor. "No! No! What have you done!?"

"You are bound, lich." Hissed the dragon. "You make one move against William, or those who are entwined with his fate, and the magic that binds your spirit to your form will be broken." Amethyst pulled her wings back. "And now I'm going to throw up..." She span around and promptly emptied her stomach into the woods, melting a large patch of ground and turning it into an evil smelling pool of steaming, bubbling, fluids.

"I hate being ill." She said, collapsing slightly.

A Guardian now

Marakel flinched as Kralla moved in behind him menacingly.

"Let go of the boy."

Immediately he let Will go. The parchment paper skin of his face was now a mask of horror. "What have you done?" He whispered, over and over as he just stood there.

Amethyst turned a bleary eye towards Will. "You are a very exhausting to be around boy. The Lich is as much a guardian now as your friend Kralla and master Tellerick. But beware. He is not your friend. Trust is earned, never bought or coerced. He may be undead, but he will help you."

He'd still be Evil

The Dragon curled up, wrapping her tail around her. "Wake me up when my ingredients arrive. I've done too much today and must sleep." And with that she closed her eyes, tilted her head and opened her mouth so she could breath properly.

Tellerick and Tamryn rounded on Marakel.

"I should put him back in the ground Tellerick." Growled Tamryn, his book of the White Saints held firmly in his paw.

"I don't think you can anymore. Amethyst has wrapped him in fate and destiny. It's thick around him."

"You could dip him in chocolate sauce, he'd still be evil."

The Augury of Destiny

Tellerick examined the shell-shocked cadaver. Most of his rotten finery had been removed by Tamryn when they'd captured him. All that remained were grave-stained shirt and long pants tucked into loose boots.

"Marakel, do you remember me?"

The Lich looked up. "Yes. She... I am fate-bound with nothing more than a word."

Tellerick nodded. "Yes, yes she did." He sighed. "Never cross a Dragon."

"What happens now?"

"Well... William is the Augury of Destiny. Now we wait. The weapons of war will come for him. We must be ready to advise them and defend ourselves and Will."

THANK YOU FOR READING